THE HERO REBELLION 0.5

HUNTER

BELINDA CRAWFORD

HENDRIX & FAUST
PUBLISHERS

Published by Hendrix & Faust, Publishers in 2020

This is a work of fiction. Names, characters, businesses, places, events, locales, and incidents are either the products of the author's imagination or used in a fictitious manner. Any resemblance to actual persons, living or dead, or actual events is purely coincidental.

www.belindacrawford.com

ISBN: 978-0-6484881-9-4 (ebook)
ISBN: 978-0-6484881-7-0 (paperback)

A catalogue record for this book is available from the National Library of Australia

Books by Belinda Crawford

The Hero Rebellion
(Hunter)
Hero
(Race)
Riven
Regan

The Echo
Cold Between Stars
Dark Between Oceans
(coming late 2020)

IN THE BEGINNING

Humans colonised Jørn; they travelled across the galaxy intent on a better way of life, away from the influence of Earth. But the drones they sent ahead, the ones that told them that Jørn was their new paradise, missed something. Something important.

The colonists arrived, settled on the surface. And started dying.

The culprit, a native spore, carried on every wind to every corner of the globe.

Genetic engineering, blending DNA from Earth and Jørn species, saved their crops and livestock, but for humans there was no cure. Instead they took to the skies, turning their five great colony ships into cities that floated above the spore's reach.

Times were hard. All the resources they bought with them to start their new lives went into the fight to stay alive. They scavenged, they scraped, they made every morsel and every scrap go as far as it could, but it was not enough.

A few brave souls risked their lives to explore the planet. They scouted the surface, locating the resources the cities needed to survive, with nothing more than the thin membrane of their envirosuits and the claws of their genetically engineered steeds to keep them alive. They died in their dozens, victims of the planet's deadly wildlife and treacherous terrain.

They became known as Riders.

Legends.

Heroes.

They did their job well, and now, two-hundred years after the first human set foot on Jørn, humans are beginning to thrive.

The era of the Riders is ending.

But not just yet.

CHAPTER ONE

Subria skidded around the corner, only her grip on the hangar's door jamb keeping her on her feet.

'Not the day to be late, Venere!' Instructor Bayard yelled over the clang of cargo and the low of giant, shaggy cow-ocs lumbering across the deck.

Subria didn't have the breath left to yell back. She let the pound of her boots do the talking, sprinting across the cavernous hangar, dodging hover sleds piled high with supplies for the new biodomes being built on the planet's surface.

It was hard to hear over the thump of her heart and the heavy *thrum* of the shuttle's engines, but she could hear her classmates' yells, even if she couldn't make out the words. They sounded urgent, frantic almost, but there was no time to figure them out, just enough to scramble up and over a hover sled, squeeze between cargo containers, leap off the other side—

And hitting the deck a second later as a cow-oc lumbered into her path. She skidded under the beast's belly, getting a new appreciation for its shaggy hide and six legs before vaulting back to her feet.

Her classmates' yells made sense a moment later. The old Morague Academy shuttle was lifting off the deck, the down rush of its engines making their own tornado.

Bayard was standing in the shuttle's open hatch, feet spread, arms crossed, the lift of her brows and the tilt of her chin challenging Subria to push harder. Or fail.

No way.

Subria pumped her legs faster.

Ten metres.

The shuttle was hovering an arm's length above the deck.

Seven metres to the open hatch.

The hatch was waist-height now.

Three metres.

This would hurt.

Two.

Chest-height.

One.

Subria leapt.

She caught the edge of the of hatch under her ribs.

Breath left her lungs in a rush, pain exploding in her belly, but there wasn't time to worry about that. No time to breathe. The ground was gone and her feet were dangling in air as the shuttle continued to rise. She hung on with her elbows, gripped the smooth deck of the shuttle with her fingers and used every muscle in her body to inch herself forwards. The instructor's shoes were right there, bulky black boots, the nano-leather scratched and scarred, dominating her vision. She didn't need to see Bayard's face to feel the weight of her gaze, didn't need to see beyond the airlock to know her classmates were there, watching, waiting. Silent now, but their tension vibrated the air.

They watched but didn't move. Help wasn't coming. On the surface, a rider had only themselves, and so she had only herself now.

She slipped.

For a second, the flight hangar flashed in her vision: the cluttered deck, the cargo crates, the other shuttles just a few metres beneath her feet. She could let go and survive, perhaps break an ankle if she didn't land properly.

But that would be failure, and she wouldn't fail. *Couldn't* fail.

Subria gritted her teeth and pulled herself up. The muscles in her shoulders screamed; her elbows, wedged against the sides of the shuttle's airlock, ground into the metal; her fingers scrambled for purchase. Slowly, so slowly every second was an hour, and her shoulder blades felt like they were going to pop out of her back and her biceps were molten strings of steelcrete, she pulled herself up. Ribs scraping against the deck, cutting into her belly, making it harder to breathe. She didn't stop. And then she was in the shuttle, the airlock's outer hatch snapping closed, cutting out the roar of the engines and the whip of the wind. Subria flopped onto her back and stared blankly at the bulkhead, dragging oxygen back into her lungs.

Then the bulkhead was gone and she was staring past green-clad legs to arms crossed over a nano-leather coat, all the way up to Bayard's flat, dark-eyed stare.

'What are you doing, Venere?'

'Breathing…ma'am,' she said between pants.

'I don't pay you to breathe, recruit.'

Subria drew another breath before replying. 'You don't pay me at all, ma'am.'

'Hmm.' She turned on her heel. 'Get off that deck.'

'Yes, ma'am.' Subria took one last second to draw in air and rolled to her feet, ignoring the dizziness that said perhaps she needed a little more oxygen before moving.

Take a beat. A memory of her daddy, his hand on her shoulder holding her steady. She took a beat. Breathed, drawing the air deep, holding it the pit of her belly, giving it time to saturate the tissues before letting it out. Head steady, she stepped into the shuttle's main cabin.

The airlock's inner door shushed shut on Subria's heels.

There were no windows in the Academy's old shuttle, but she knew when they dropped out of the shuttle bay and into the sky below Cumulus City by the lurch as they left the city's mag-net behind.

Subria gripped the nearest seat.

A row of hard seats ran down both sides of the cabin, enough for forty recruits, let alone the eight that were there.

A decade ago, before the new biodomes were built on Jørn's surface, the shuttle would have been crammed with recruits. The cities almost didn't need riders to scout resources anymore; the biodomes had seen to that, freeing up resources for the engineers and scientists to do things like build better shuttles.

But it was Subria's dream. She didn't care about the credits, or the kudos. Jørn's surface was in her blood, and spending her life in the cities, floating kilometres above the ground, wasn't.

Her older sister thought she was mad, but then, anything that involved dirt made Husna cringe, and her mum…

Her mum had stared hard at the Morague Academy application, expression carefully blank, but she'd gripped the kitchen bench hard enough to whiten her knuckles and make the holo-chef flicker.

'A rider,' she'd said, and there'd been something in her tone that reminded Subria of brittle plasglas a second from breaking.

Subria had straightened her spine. 'I need your signature.'

Her mum had looked up, and it'd taken every last bit of will not to step back. There'd been fire in her mum's dark eyes, an inferno of pain and pent-up rage, of old memories and newer nightmares, nightmares Subria shared. It was enough that it should have burned through her mum's pale gold skin and seared Subria's retinas.

She remembered the way sweat had trickled down her spine, the burning urge to shift her feet and to fiddle with the stylus she'd carefully placed beside her application.

'You know what it means if I sign this.' It hadn't been a question.

Subria had nodded. 'Yes,' she'd said.

Her mum's jaw had tightened, lips compressing into a thin line, and she'd stared hard at the stylus, as if she could crush it by thought alone. She snatched it off the bench. 'Anything but Farm Control,' her mum had said as she signed the application.

Anything but the job that had killed her dad, even if the alternative was the one responsible for the white lumps of scar tissue and the limp her mum would never talk about.

Subria could live with that.

She made her way between the rows to the back of the shuttle, pushing aside the plasglas that separated the main cabin from the smaller one behind, shutting out the soft whispers as she slid it closed behind her. The back compartment took up a third of the shuttle, but it was empty now, except for the small crate secured in the shelving of the bulkhead.

The crate was what she wanted. Subria deactivated the mag-lock keeping it in place, pulling it out and setting it on the deck.

It was heavy for its size, although most of that was the thick black plasform, reinforced with a super thin layer of steelcrete, the only material strong enough to resist Erberos' talons. Her thumb on the top of the crate activated the control pad, and eight digits disengaged the four steelcrete rods holding the door closed.

She held her hand in front of the crate, palm up, and waited.

The door stood open for several long heartbeats, and she thought Erberos had escaped again, somehow twisted his nimble little paws through the holes in the plasform and bypassed the thumb lock to tap in the code. How it was possible she didn't have a clue, but she'd seen the wan-adder do stranger things.

She was bending down, canting sideways to peer into the crate, when a shadow slinked out of its depths.

Light was needed to really see Erberos, to make out more than the slim, lithe outline of the wan-adder as he stepped onto her hand and wound his way up her arm. There wasn't enough of it in the shuttle – was barely enough under the full, blazing light of her sister's lab, where he'd been made.

His sleek, sharp muzzle kissed the nape of her neck before the last of him was out of the crate, the wicked claws on his nimble forepaws sinking into the thick nano-leather of her coat, tips pricking her skin. The claws matched the teeth crammed into his narrow, triangular head, sharper and deadlier than an animal his size had a right to, the gleaming white tips the only points of brightness in his otherwise black body. Even his eyes, all four of them, were dark.

'Pitiless pools,' her sister once said. 'As dark and merciless as his soul.'

Subria had scratched Erebos's head, finding the spot behind his right ear with the tip of her nail, causing the little flyer to close his eyes in bliss. 'He's a sweetheart,' she'd said.

Her sister, older than her by over a decade, had scoffed. 'He's the Devil little sister, and he'll steal *your* soul just because he can.'

She reached up and scratched that same ear now, smiling at the sibilant purr that vibrated through his throat. 'You aren't going steal my soul, are you?'

Erebos rubbed his head under her jaw, his scales warm and silken against her skin, and purred louder.

Subria smiled and, still scratching his ear, returned to the main cabin.

'Heads up, the shadow beast is out!' The words cut through the hubbub of conversation, said in the joking-but-not tone she'd come to expect from Tyvian.

She flicked the boy a glance but didn't acknowledge him. Jealousy wasn't a good look on Tyvian Joshi. It pinched the skin around the leaf-green of his eyes and twisted his mouth, as if he'd sucked a cherry-lemon. Fear looked even worse, and he wore both expressions. He tried to hide them, covering up the fear with jest and the jealousy with a smile, but she saw it in his eyes, eyes that were stuck on Erebos, longing and nightmares in their depths.

She brushed past him, noticed the way he twitched, like he didn't know whether to flinch or snatch Erebos from around her neck, and felt…satisfaction.

She saw her dad in her mind's eye, the downwards cast of his face, the disappointment he would have felt if he'd known, if he'd been alive to know, the way the satisfaction slithered through her chest, warm and sleek.

Subria shook it away. Satisfaction at the expense of another was an ugly emotion, unworthy.

Sinful.

Her dad wouldn't have approved, would have looked at her with that half-frown between his eyes, the one that was felt more than seen: a solid punch below the heart. The kind that reminded her of the duty, responsibility and privilege that came from being a Venere.

Erebos's tail wrapped through her fingers. She caught the tip. Maybe the little shadow *was* stealing her soul. Part of her didn't care, but the bigger part, the one that remembered the way disappointment would shadow her dad's eyes, did.

⊕

It was a long ride to the Farm on the shuttle's hard seats. By the time the pitch of the engines changed, climbed for a heartbeat before cutting out altogether, Subria's legs were stiff and her bum sore.

Instructor Bayard sat at the front of the cabin, a few seats away from the recruits, but it might as well have been miles.

There was a shudder and a gentle *clunk* as they landed. A ripple of excitement passed through the recruits.

Instructor Bayard stood.

The shuttle fell silent. Tension shivered through the deck.

'This is your hardest exam. There are no right answers, no strategies. The bond between rider and companion cannot be taught, forced or willed into existence.' The instructor stalked the aisles, eyeing each of them in turn. 'Some of you will find such a bond, some of you won't.' She stopped in front of Subria, looked her in the eye. 'There is no shame in failure.'

Subria stroked Erebos.

Bayard kept walking. 'The surface doesn't give you second chances, and neither do its creations, no matter how much of Old Terra we put into them. If you do not return to this shuttle with a companion, you'll be packing your bags and going home.'

A hush filled the silence in the wake of the instructor's words.

Bayard stopped in front of the airlock, the door cycling open behind her. 'Welcome to the Farm.'

CHAPTER TWO

'Welcome to the Farm!' The man's smile split his dark face. 'We're on level three, just below the site where the very first colonists made landfall.'

'Uh...' Canavan's hand rose in the wave of his voice. '...sir? The first colonists landed on Englic in the Petal Plain.'

The man laughed, pale green lab coat flaring about his knees as he spun around. 'Not so, Recruit...?' Perhaps it was the way the man stuck his finger in the air, the imperious rigidity of it, the way the fat silver sheath encasing it from knuckle to middle joint flashed in the light flooding through the wall of plasglas, but no one laughed as he swung back around to face them.

'Uh... Canavan, sir.'

'Recruit Canavan!' The man must be a spinning top, Subria thought, as he completed another turn. Once facing away from them again, he marched towards the big double doors, boots *cracking* on the shiny floor. 'It's a common mistake, Recruit Canavan. While the bulk of the colonists *did* land in the Petal Plains, the first *actual* human to set foot on Jørn soil did so right *here*.'

He spun again, feet coming together with a *snap*, forcing Subria to jerk to a halt before she ran into him. Her back wasn't so lucky, and she winced as someone rammed a datapad between her shoulder blades.

She didn't turn to see who it was, barely heard the mumbled 'sorry'. There was some kind of weird power about the man's finger, the way he held it stiff and straight, pointed towards the ceiling, that transfixed her, left her unable to tear her gaze from the shiny ring.

'Actually,' he said, leaning close and lowering his voice. 'It was twelve point eight metres that way.' He motioned upwards, and Subria's eyes followed, looking straight up at the ceiling along with the rest of her classmates.

Maybe it wasn't his finger; maybe the power was in the flash of his too-white teeth against the dark umber of his face. The twinkle in his eyes, the hint of a secret, a joke buried in their depths? Perhaps it was all of those, or maybe it was a magnet in that damned ring, calibrated not to metal but overeager recruits.

Whatever it was, it was a lodestone in her gut, bending her spine, drawing her eyes, stretching her hearing so she wouldn't miss a single word. She felt Canavan, Bank and Elstra draw closer behind her, crowding up against her back. The other recruits huddled in at her sides, the ring sucking them all in.

The metal gleamed silver. She never wanted to take her eyes from it, never wanted to—

A ringing in her ears, the sharp piercing sound reaching into her brain, winding around neurones and telling her to let go. A loud *click* sounded somewhere deep inside.

Subria jerked upright.

'Temple!' The name snapped though the foyer, a laser driving away the last of the ring's magnetic pull.

'Stop playing with my recruits,' the same voice said.

'Ursula!' The man's – Temple's? – smile changed. 'How nice to see you.'

Instructor Bayard didn't waste a word, but something radiated off her with every *snap* of her boots. Not anger, exactly, not disgust either, but something else, a sense that reminded Subria of a predator stalking larger prey, like a skunk-wolf pursuing a pea-dragon.

Wariness.

Subria shifted her feet. Bayard's watchfulness settled in her spine, making her look at the scientist, at Temple, with sharper eyes.

'No hug?' The scientist spread his hands, teeth gleaming.

Bayard crossed her arms. 'Just get on with it.'

'Of course, of course.' Temple turned, his hands coming together, not quite rubbing with glee. His gaze caught Subria's, seemed to pick her out of the recruits and held on. Then again, he might have seen Erebos wrapped around her neck.

Nevertheless, Temple's grin stretched to its original cheek-splitting size, and he gestured them to move towards the big lift doors at the back. Subria had the notion that Doctor Temple looked at her deliberately, had sought her out of the crowd. The thought made her shudder, and for a second it was as if a worm slid out of Temple's eyes and into her soul. A prayer was whispering from her lips, her hand starting to make a cross over her chest, before she clenched her fist and chided herself for letting her imagination take hold.

Erberos shifted, the soft warmth of his tail tightening around her biceps.

Temple's attention turned away, and she knew that he hadn't seen Erberos before, that the 'adder had only now lifted his head out of the concealment of her hair, by the alarm that stole across the doctor's features. It was there and then gone, replaced by a considering look that slithered through her insides.

'Follow me, then.' Temple gestured behind him, and was it her imagination, or did he speak directly to her? 'Into the bowels of the Farm we go.'

A shiver ran down Subria's spine.

⊕

The lift opened, and for several shocked seconds, Subria's brain struggled to believe the evidence of her eyes. A forest spread out before them, a dozen paces of pale steelcrete separating the lift from a swarth of grass so green it hurt her eyes. The grass disappeared into a line of trees, thin trunks and spindly branches reaching towards a blue sky.

Her classmates brushed past her, out onto the half-moon of steelcrete, murmurs of wonder rippling between them. She followed them out and turned, taking in the lift, standing all on its own amidst the intense green, following it up and up and up until it disappeared into the sky, blue studded with fluffy clouds.

She should be panicking; the thought was clear as a bell. She should be holding her breath and running for the safety of the lift before the spore that saturated Jørn's lower atmosphere infested her lungs.

Take a beat. Her dad's words rang in her memory.

It was probably already too late, another, sane part of her pointed out. Panic would make her breathe harder, draw more toxin in, and besides… Instructor Bayard wasn't wearing an enviromask.

Her gazed sharpened on a hint of static rippling through the perfect clouds.

The holograms were good, really good, she thought as she brought her attention back down. It would have been better if they'd muted the colours and tweaked the enviros to produce a breeze, added the sweet scent of grass and the dustier one of wet soil. If they had, she'd have doubted her sanity, been reaching for an enviromask, or, like Bank, dashing for the lift, before she got Pollen poisoning.

Instructor Bayard stepped aside as Bank hit the lift, frantically stabbing the controls, terror in the frantic looks over his shoulder.

'Come on!' He screamed the words, and Subria wondered if it was at his classmates or the lift's closed doors. They opened, and he dashed inside, jabbing at the controls there. 'Come on,' he yelled again. 'Before we all get Pollen poisoning!'

'Uh.' Canavan stepped forward, his hand outstretched and face twisted in an expression that was alarmed but sheepish at the same time, as if he too had experienced the moment of panic that gripped Bank in its talons. 'Bank, it's just a—'

Instructor Bayard held up a hand, forestalling him, and glanced around the set of the recruits. 'Does anyone wish to join Recruit

Bank?' No one moved.

Bank stopped jabbing at the control pad, and his eyes widened to saucers in his pale face, his mouth dropping open, and Subria guessed logic was finally taking over from the blind rush of adrenalin.

He started to step out of the lift, but Instructor Bayard pushed him back.

'That's a fail, Mr Bank. See you at the shuttle.'

'But—'

The doors closed.

Subria stared at them, at the way they reflected the holographic forest, capturing it under the milk-white skin of the plascrete and bouncing the scene back.

That had been… Unexpected. Strange. Worthy of consideration. She stroked Erebos's tail, wrapped around her bicep.

Something wasn't right here, and it was more than Doctor Temple's ring.

Bayard crossed her arms. 'Temple, I believe you can dispense with the… ' Her mouth twisted with distaste as she gestured at the forest.

The doctor beamed. 'Yes, of course.' A click of his fingers, the huge ring encasing his index finger flashing. 'Time to get to the main show.'

The forest vanished, and the urge to duck hit Subria so hard, her hands were halfway over her head before she checked the movement.

Embarrassment surged up her cheeks, and she scowled, even as she darted looks at her classmates to check if any of them noticed her nerves.

A sheepish glance from a half-crouched Canavan told her she hadn't been the only one, while a smirk from Tyvian had her cheeks flaming brighter and her scowl deepening.

She straightened, pulling the ends of her jacket down and lifting her chin.

Where there had been trees and sky, there were now off-white walls and a ceiling that stretched high overhead. But none of that was what captured her attention. No, that was all for the twelve huge striders waiting behind the doctor.

Five different species of the riding companions waited next to their handlers. The pea-dragon was the smallest, with its long graceful neck and sleek, scaled body, half-covered with brilliant plumage. Its back would only come up to Subria's breast bone, even if its head towered over her.

The sternards, on the other hand… There were five of the great beasts, each one a tower of muscle and fur, their chests platted with heavy scales that ran under their bellies and crested their blocky heads, running from the tips of their big black noses to the ends of their stubby tails. They loomed over their handlers and made the dober-shepherds, the same height but sleek and lithe, seem small.

'Recruits.' Bayard's voice rang through the silence. The instructor stepped out in front of the group, into the centre of the semi-circle made by the stablehands and striders. 'Riders do not pick their companions, at least not in whole. Whether or not you walk out of here with a strider at your side is not up to you, but to the stablehands and companions beside them. Your test starts now.'

The recruits scattered.

Subria took one stumbling, half-step forwards before her gaze caught on the companion standing at the end of the curving line, apart from the others.

Erebos growled, too low for Subria to hear, but she felt it, running through her blood, turning it cold.

No other human noticed, but the ruc-pard did.

The blue-grey animal swung its gaze to Subria.

Her heart froze. The animal was huge, taller than the sternards, but where they were mountains of muscle, the 'pard exuded danger and death. Its blue-grey coat shone under the lights, gleaming in shades of silver and violet, while its black hairless tail swished from side-to-side. Wicked claws were sheathed at the end of its six long, muscular legs, and unbidden came the memory of how they looked soaked in blood, how they tore flesh.

The animal gaze caught Subria's, deep and dark, pulling her forwards—

Erebos hissed, the sound jerking her out of the 'pard's gaze.

Air shuddered into her lungs, and she spun away, staring blindly in the opposite direction, fighting the memory of a dark, dead forest and blood. It rang in her head, the sickening *crunch,* the hot, metallic scent.

Erebos hummed, his tail wrapping tighter around her bicep. The prick of his claws bringing her attention back to him.

His forepaws were propped on the leather pad over her shoulder, lifting himself upright on his forepaws while the rest of him remained draped around her neck.

She concentrated on breathing, on Erebos's tail wrapped around her arm, his paws kneading her shoulder, the rustle of his wings. She focused on all of that, using it to push the darkness away, behind the thin shield of denial. Prayed it would hold.

Instructor Bayard was watching her, the older woman's expression considering. Subria imagined the dark gaze peeling back the layers of her skull, peering inside and prying out her nightmares.

She looked away, caught a glimpse of Doctor Temple disappearing down a dark corridor, and fell into huge caramel eyes set in a broad blunt face. Subria forgot about the scent of blood and decay, about the ruc-pard, and saw only the honey-coloured sternard.

Her feet moved of their own accord. One moment she was in front of the lift, the next she was surrounded by the musky scent of fur and the warmth radiating from the sternard.

'This is Yaara.' A woman Subria hadn't seen spoke. 'But I don't think you two need an introduction.' The handler grinned at Subria's outstretched hand, the one she didn't remember lifting.

She snatched the limb back.

'Sorry,' she said, forcing herself to look at the woman, even though everything in her itched to stroke Yaara's big, hairy nose.

It wasn't just rude to touch another's companion without

permission; it was dangerous. She knew that well enough; Erebos wasn't shy about sinking fangs and talons into those stupid enough to forget. Like she'd just done.

And yet, she couldn't help reaching out again, wondering if Yaara's fur was as soft and deep as it looked.

'I just…' Her attention drifted back to the sternard, and she heard rather than saw the smile in the handler's voice.

'I get it, kid, but you're safe enough with this girl. She wouldn't hurt a fly.'

Her breath caught in her chest as the sternard reached back, dipping her great blocky head, angling it so Subria's hand slipped behind her ear. The breath left her chest, and her heart stopped as her fingers sank into Yaara's pelt. It was *softer*, warmer and thicker than… than—

Yaara butted her in the chest.

From somewhere far off, the handler laughed and said, 'Breathe, kid.'

Subria took a deep, shuddering breath, the sweet, warm scent of Yaara's fur soaking the air.

Erebos slid out from under her hair, a sleek shadow resting his forepaws on her bicep, his double wings half-mantled, his neck arched and all four eyes locked on Yaara.

Subria held her breath, thought the handler did the same.

The sternard rolled big brown eyes, almost as big as Erebos's head. The strider could eat the little flyer in one bite and pick her teeth with the shards of Subria's bones, if she wanted. The only companion more dangerous than an angry sternard was the blue-grey ruc-pard in the corner, the one whose gaze she could feel boring into her back.

Carefully, Subria started to pull away, feeling the loss in her bones as keenly as the embarrassment for letting herself get carried away, for not *thinking*. If Erebos decided to attack—

The flyer crooned and, quick as a linch-adder, leapt from Subria's arm to wrap himself around Yaara's head and rub his jaw between her ears.

She snapped her mouth closed. 'I think he likes her.'

'Yeah.' The handler grinned again. 'Well, congrats, kid. That's got to be one of the fastest bondings I've ever seen, although I will admit, when that flyer came out from under your hair, I thought we might have a problem—'

Pain exploded in Subria's ears.

CHAPTER THREE

Subria dropped to her knees.

She had no breath to scream. There was only the pain in her head, drilling through her ears in a high-pitched whine, digging through bone and skin until it reached her brain. It split, lightning under her skull, wrapping around her brain with electric fingers, digging into the grey matter like it was searching for something.

What? She wanted to ask. *What do you want?*

She'd have given anything for it to stop, just for a second, a heartbeat. Half a heartbeat.

Distantly, she was aware of Yaara's handler crashing to the ground, of Erebos taking flight, talons leaving rents in her jacket.

She couldn't think. There was only feeling left, only the pain, that excruciating lance digging and scraping and searching some more.

Her sight was fading, the stables blurring at the edges, going white as her entire being narrowed down to the sound, to the pain. There was nothing else, no room for anything else. The sound was in every bit of her, under her skin, in her blood, bound to the pain, twisting and turning until she couldn't tell where one began and the other ended.

It was in her DNA; her genetics changing, the molecules splitting and reforming, making new patterns, and she knew that for the rest of her life, however long that was, the screech would equal pain.

There was no stable anymore, no grass or steelcrete, no handler passed out by her side or honey-coloured sternard in her face. Just the inside of her eyelids. It took several moments for it to sink into her pores, for her to recognise it. She heard nothing, not the beat of her heart, the harsh draw of her breath. Nothing.

It was... beautiful. Heavenly.

In the pit of her being, something *clicked*.

After the silence, the sound rang through her skull. Loud. Sharp. The vibration shook her bones, shivering her skin. Ringing. Ringing. Ringing. Other sounds came with it. The *thump thump thump* of her pulse, the drag of air through her nose and into her lungs. The ear-shredding screech.

Except it didn't shred her ears anymore, didn't bring pain. It just...screeched. A low-pitched siren on the edge of her hearing, the distant sound of nails on chalkboard, twitching her skin.

It was nothing.

And yet...there was something under her skin, a vibration to counter the noise. It shivered and danced, mixing with the screech, reaching for it and becoming something else, something powerful.

Subria blinked, vision clearing, walls and floors coming into focus, sensations pinging on her consciousness. The hard floor under her knees, leeching warmth from her bones, the trickle of sweat down the side of her face. Her hands, palms pressed to the floor. The taste of copper on her lips, the sticky, cooling puddle in the spread of her fingers, bright red and shiny. A matching drop formed on the tip of her nose, the liquid she'd thought was sweat rolling into a thick, heavy ball before falling in slow motion.

Subria breathed, a great shuddering gasp, and now the sweet, salty taste on her lips made sense.

She shot to her feet. Stumbled as she backpedalled.

Blood, a swath of it spilled across the white floor.

How—? 'Oh, God.'

The prayer rang in her head as her every neurone froze at the sight of Yaara's handler.

The woman sprawled at Subria's feet, eyes and mouth open, her throat ripped out, a bloody mess of red meat and the silky, translucent gleam of tendon.

Vomit burned Subria's throat, exploded out of her mouth, landing in a doubly sickening *plop* in the blood, drawing another heave out of her stomach.

Bent at the waist, she heaved a third time. Tears pooled in her eyes. She waited for a fourth, and when nothing came, she wiped her mouth, trying to ignore the sticky strings of congealing blood mixing with the stomach acid and spit on her sleeve. *Wanting* to ignore it, but still, some part of her needed to know.

She dragged a hand across her cheek, through the warmth she'd though was sweat. Her hand came away bloody.

Another wave of nausea rose from her gut, but Subria swallowed it.

Slowly, careful not to slip in blood, she turned.

Bodies littered the stables, human and companion alike. She thought most of them moved, small muscles twitching in their faces, limbs jerking, chests rising and falling, and no more pools of blood.

Pressure lifted from Subria's heart, made it easier to breathe, even if that breath wanted to shudder and jerk, to tear out of her body on a sob. She fought it, wrapped her arms around her middle and squeezed tight.

Take a beat, little tiger. The memory of her dad's voice, clear and warm despite her visor's echoing comms, steadied her.

"Take a beat,' she whispered to herself. 'And *think*.'

Something had knocked all the humans out, but... there weren't enough companions lying on the floor.

The pea-dragon was there, half-covering Tyvian with its wings, the spideruck next to it, and there, the black and tan of the dober-shepherds, and next to them the great shaggy hides of four sternards... But no ruc-pard.

She turned around all the way, trying not to look at the woman and her pool of blood.

And no Yaara, neither hide nor hair, only bloody paw prints the size of her head, leading away.

Panic bubbled along with the acid in her gut, while nightmares played at the edges of her memory. She said another prayer under her breath.

She needed a rifle. The thought was still ringing in her head when a shadow moved in the corner of her vision.

She spun, nightmares momentarily transforming the stable into a long-abandoned park, populating it with the slim trunks of trees, branches denuded of leaves, covering the floor with a layer of grass and dead foliage that crackled under her feet.

The shadow stepped out of the hallucination, and for a moment the sharp muzzle and bloodied fangs filled her vision.

Subria scrambled backwards.

Her sight cleared, the old park giving way to the clean, bright lines of The Farm's stables, the bloody muzzle emerging out of the darkness becoming Yaara's broad, blunt head, lips pulled back from her teeth, her eyes liquid pools of madness.

Red soaked Yaara's chin, ran down her throat and coated the thick plates of her chest. Head dipping low as she crouched, tension gathering in her shoulders as she prepared to leap.

Subria backed away, first one sidelong step and then another, her back to the wall.

The beast kept pace, one giant paw following the other. Silent but for the gentle *snick* of its claws, hidden within the golden hair of its toes.

One step. Another paw lifted and laid down.

Another.

A shape leaped between them, blue-grey and muscular, with a long hairless tail lashing from side to side.

The ruc-pard.

Fear turned cold and hard in her gut.

Subria fell as her feet caught something warm, soft and moving, landing hard on her butt, hands slamming into the hard floor, eyes stuck on the twin mountains of muscles, fur and fangs. Nightmares knocked on the back of her brain, bleeding through the walls she'd worked long and hard to erect against them. Crawling into her ears, into her eyes, feeding off the screech, off the *click,* and suddenly, the body under her legs, the one she'd stumbled over, wasn't warm and breathing, didn't have Canavan's sandy hair, but her dad's black buzz.

A thick tail slapped Subria back to reality, and suddenly she had an up-close-and-personal view of the 'pard's belly, the fur white. For a second her heart rose in her throat, threatening to choke her. Subria's lungs burned, shock overriding adrenalin, switching off her brain, leaving only the strange mix of wonder and fear behind. Another snarl ripped through the stable, low and ugly, the kind of sound made by something with big teeth and longer claws. Subria's heart dropped, letting oxygen back in, self-preservation with it. She scuttled backwards on hands and bum. For some reason her attention remained fix on the belly above, the way the pale grey narrowed, the fur becoming thicker and longer as she crab-walked back and back and back... And then she was on the other side of the stable, or the companion moved again, or she blacked out, because one moment there was a strider above her and the next... the next yowls and snarls rode the air, the sounds full of blood and violence.

Sternard and ruc-pard rolled across the stable, blue-grey mixing with honey, breaking apart, snarling, clashing again. Around and around, Yaara dancing amongst the bodies, the ruc-pard pushing her out of their reach. A bright red arch, erupting from the tangle, the hot, coppery stench of blood mixing with the musk and dirt of the striders.

Again and again they broke apart and clashed, stalking each other in endless circles.

Blood flew, a bright red arc. Yaara roared. The 'pard lunged, its muzzle stained red, jaws open, claws the size of Subria's face flashing on the end of four of its six legs, all of it reaching for the sternard, a blue-grey wall of muscle and fury. Of death and blood.

For a second, as the 'pard flew through the air and Yaara braced herself for the attack, Subria froze, fascinated. In that second, the world slowed, and the two great beasts – muscles bunching, teeth bared – came together in a slow-motion dance of violence. The 'pard's claws sank into Yaara's sides, one paw skidding over the thick scales of her chest, the others finding flesh, the 'pard's teeth doing the same.

Instead of evading, Yaara leapt into the attack, her own jaws – twice as heavy – open wide.

The two beasts met, chest to chest. More blood, the coppery scent of it saturating the air.

Even with the other animal's jaws clamped onto its neck, Yaara forced the 'pard backwards, her powerful hide-quarters bunching and releasing, forelegs grappling with the 'pard.

The screech of claws over the steelcrete broke Subria out of her trance.

She surged to her feet as, with a twist and a push, Yaara threw the 'pard into a wall and came for her.

She was sprinting for the lift before her heart had time to squeeze.

The sternard was faster.

One second Yaara was behind her, the next the companion was between her and safety, massive blocky head lowered, lips pulled back from red gums, the hot stink of violence on her breath.

Subria's daddy's words rang in her memory, not that last pain-filled scream, but the steady calm, guiding her out of danger. 'Prey is fast and jerky, predators are slow and smooth. Don't be prey, no matter how hard your heart beats or adrenalin runs in your body. Never be the prey.'

Slowly, her gaze steady on the space between the sternard's eyes, she backed up.

Yaara kept pace.

Madness swam in her eyes, the deep, soulful, caramel gaze washed away under... what? The screech?

Behind the sternard were the lifts and escape. But if she left, what was to stop Yaara from tearing into her classmates and the handlers?

The handlers. Her memory flicked back, recalling the weapons strapped to their waists. She backed up another step, her foot colliding with something small and black, sending it skidding across the floor. Subria took her eyes off Yaara, just a split second, just long enough to identify the pistol, but it was enough for Yaara's posture to change, for her muscles to bunch.

Smooth and steady wasn't going to cut it.

She dived for the pistol, arms out, every fibre *reaching*.

Belly hitting the ground, air leaving her lungs, a dark honey-coloured shadow rising over her back. Sliding on her stomach, fingers closing over plasform, the electric hum as the pistol reacted to her touch, barrel forming out of the grip. Rolling, energy gathering at the end of the weapon. No need to aim, not with those jaws coming for her head. The *snap* as she fired.

Yaara collapsed.

There was a split-second, time enough for realisation to dawn, for Subria to tense, before the mountain of muscle and fur came down.

She tried to roll, got halfway onto her side, arm flung out as if she could grab at the air, when several hundred kilos of sternard buried her.

Nose flattened against steelcrete, Yaara crushing her lungs. Subria struggled to breathe, struggled to lift her head, to wriggle, to move. Black was taking over her vision, her chest burned, and—

The weight was gone.

The first breath was magic, filling her from the inside out. On the second, she surged to her knees, came face-to-snout with the ruc-pard.

Eyes the colour of obsidian met hers, and Subria fell.

⊕

There was no gravity, no time, no cold, no blood. Fear and adrenalin dropped away, leaving a curious weightlessness, a sense of waiting and… something else.

Discomfort rippled through her chest, a stretching on the inside of her ribs, gentle at first and then stronger, verging on the edge of pain. There was a new space next to her heart, or maybe *in* her heart, as if something were trying to make a new home. Then a knocking, reverberating through her chest, reaching out with silver fingers. Behind it... she didn't know what it was, but it felt like someone saying 'hello'.

Subria jerked back into her own body, surging to her feet, putting as much distance between herself and the ruc-pard as she could.

Her chest still rang with the knocking, and the space behind her heart was still there, cramping her lungs, shortening her breath, but it had stopped growing, stopped trying to send tendrils of... of emotion through her body. But still...

The 'pard rumbled, cocking her head to the side, her eyes beckoning Subria closer, promising... promising... she didn't know what, but it was huge, life-changing, like everything she'd ever wanted and hadn't known. Like destiny.

Subria leaned forwards.

Darkness descended on four sleek wings, sucking in the light, only to flash it out again from talons and fangs. Erberos snarled, the sound slicing through the air, sliding into her ears, a knife so sharp there wasn't any pain.

The 'pard flattened her ears and backed away from the wan-adder with a snarl of her own, bloodied lips pulling back from bloodied teeth.

'Venere.' The sound of her name, the familiar voice scratchy and threaded with pain, broke the tension, snapped Subria's gaze to the dark shape slumped against the wall.

'Instructor Bayard.' She was at the older woman's side in moments, Erebos clinging to her shoulder, the ruc-pard a shadow in the corner of her eye.

The instructor's head and shoulders were propped against the wall, the rest of her sprawled on the floor. Subria bent to help her up, but Bayard pushed her hands away.

'No time.' Grabbing Subria's jacket, Bayard tugged until her lips brushed against Subria's ear. 'He's gone for the gene banks. Stop him. Follow the sound.'

The fingers in Subria's jacked loosened and fell away as Bayard lost consciousness.

CHAPTER FOUR

She stalked the hallways alone, pistol gripped in both hands and pointed at the floor, steps smooth and slow.

Follow the sound. Instructor Bayard's last words shivered in her memory.

The sound vibrated in her skull until she wasn't sure if it was in her ears or in her bones.

It led her deep into the bowels of the Farm, past the stables and through heavy doors left ajar, into a barracks filled with narrow hallways and more people slumped over chairs and workbenches, others sprawled on the floor. She checked them all, stopped to feel the pulse in their necks, even though the urgency of Bayard's command ran through her head, made her skin tight with the need to *move.*

Stalk and check and stalk again. At some point the lights changed, the bright daylight replaced with the demonic red glow of emergency lights.

The tension in her shoulders became a ball of dread.

On her shoulder, Erebos flexed his claws.

The corridor branched, and she paused, debating which way to go. Both branches looked the same in the eerie emergency glows, filled with shadows as impenetrable as Erebos's hide. Tension grew out of the nerves crawling up her back, ran down her arms in sweaty rivulets.

Follow the sound.

Subria skirted around the corner, pistol still held low, back to the wall.

Follow the sound.

The ache of her teeth, the pound of blood between calcium and flesh, lessened with every step, the awful screech in her eardrums going with it. Subria hadn't realised how much it hurt, how tightly she'd been gritting her jaw, until the pressure eased. For a handful of steps, it was blissful. Then: *Shit.*

She was going the wrong way.

Subria spun, slinked back the way she'd come, boots still silent on the plascrete, heel gliding to toe, always aware, always watchful. She imagined her daddy slinking along beside her, remembered the last time he'd taken her hunting; the quiet in and out of his breathing through the comms in her ear.

'Heel and toe, baby girl. Mind the debris, but keep your focus on the 'pard. Breathe easy, heart slow, hand steady. He'll smell your fear if you let him, hear your heartbeat if it rises.'

Except there was no 'pard to stalk. The 'pard was back in the foyer, watching over her classmates, and that thought… that thought made her shiver, brought the nightmare closer to the surface. Her gut curled in on itself, her breath came in short, hard jerks, and the deep gurgling scream filled her ears—

Subria pushed it away, focused on the sharp stab of Erebos's claws, the ache in her gums, the screech vibrating through her skull, pounding at her ears, louder and louder with every gliding step down the corridor. Slowly, painfully, the nightmare, the scream, retreated.

Erebos growled, scales warm on her neck, driving a wedge of darkness between the nightmares and her.

She kept going. Heel and toe. Heel and toe.

The hallway changed, the space narrowing. Still dark, but the red glows on the walls were getting closer, becoming a funnel, until the glow was all around, distorting the shadows, making them shallow where they should have been deep. What was this place? The hallway was long, she could have reached out and touched either side without straining. There were no outlines of doors, no darker shadows to suggest other hallways, only the red shadows and the ache in her jaw to lead her on.

A plasglas door, planted in the middle of the hall, standing open. She hesitated, wondered for a moment if this was wise, if Instructor Bayard had really meant Subria to follow the sound, or if that was something she'd *thought* she'd heard. But then why the pistol? Why that whisper that tumbled from her lips as the instructor slid to the ground?

Why?

Her dad's voice played in her memory, his hand on her shoulder. 'Focus on the ruc-pard, little girl, not the end, the means or the warrant in your pocket. Just the 'pard, only the 'pard.'

Focus on the 'pard. On the ache in her jaw, on the purpose in Instructor Bayard's eyes, the determination and that tiny, tiny flicker of fear.

Focus. The whys would take care of themselves when the job was done.

She padded past the door, taking note of the big black letters stenciled on the plasglas, questions bubbling up in her gut at the meaning, but she pushed them back. Later.

Focus.

The hallway ended with a body on the floor and another door, wedged open by the body. Slowly, eyes and ears alert to the shadows, Subria knelt, feeling with one hand for a pulse. The dark made it difficult, that and the new itch at her nape, the one that said if she took her eyes off the door, she wasn't getting up again.

Erebos slithered over her shoulder, his weight creeping down her bicep. He paused there, waiting.

'Fly,' she whispered, never taking her eyes from the door.

He launched upwards, double wings beating hard and silent.

She rose, pistol up, as he disappeared into shadows and slipped through the gap between wall and door. More darkness, although this one not leavened by the red of emergency lights.

Enough light slipped through the door for her to make out the darker well not two meters beyond, and the bulky shape of a hand rail.

Stairs.

Down, down, down she went. She didn't hear the screech anymore, but it vibrated in her jaw, filled it with a bone-deep ache that grew with every step.

The stairs ended at another door, open like the last. No bodies here, just a small vestibule and an airlock, standing open, and... databanks.

She came out of the airlock and into a forest of databanks, gelpacks filling the darkness with soft blue light.

Glowing sentinels in the darkness, lining the circular walls, standing silent watch around a column of pale blue, lit from within by shards of lightning. An AI core, circled by the soft glow of an active workstation. And there, a silhouette against the light, was a person.

'Stop him.' Instructor Bayard's voice, the flicker of fear, ran through Subria's mind.

Boots silent on the steelcrete, Subria slinked closer. The pistol came up of its own volition, a holographic crosshair popping to life over the barrel.

Heel to toe. Breathing steady, heart slow. The calm settled over her, syncing breath and movement, slowing her heart and narrowing her focus until all she saw was the target on the man's back.

'You have a remarkable resistance to sonic disruption, Ms Venere. Most lose consciousness, a few hallucinate, but I've never seen someone keep functioning.' The silhouette spoke without turning, his hands on the workstation, shifting through holoscreens. She knew that voice, recognised the timbre of it even without the animation of his cheek-splitting smile. 'Is it training? Your father was a remarkable man, almost a match for your mother, in fact. It would not have surprised me if he followed me down here, dead as he is.'

Shock rippled under her calm, threatened to make its way to her skin, at the mention of her parents, at the familiarity in Temple's tone. He'd known her dad?

The doctor turned, and there was his smile, not splitting his cheeks, but smaller, secretive. 'But I don't think it's training. Kylian Venere had a lifetime of it and, as I recall, some damage to his hearing, which would have made his resistance to my disruptor plausible. My guess is you've somehow adapted to the frequency, a slight adjustment should fix that.' Temple lifted his hands, seeming to notice the pistol for the first time, the ring on his left hand gleamed in the gelpacks' light.

'You're not going to shoot me now, are you, Ms Venere?'

Subria stopped, feet planted, weight spread, and her hands rock steady on the pistol, like her daddy taught.

Temple's brow lifted. 'I see you have your father's way with words, rather than your mother's.' He lifted his arms, a question forming in his posture. 'What would you like me to do? Surrender? For what? Do you even know what I'm doing down here?'

The calm that had settled over her shoulders shivered, doubt worming its way through the memory of her daddy whispering instructions. She'd never held a pistol on a person before. Never. Never. Never. The hint of a tremor moved the barrel.

She licked her lips. 'What are you doing down here, Doctor?'

The smile on his face bloomed. 'Would you believe that I'm maintaining the databanks?'

'No.'

His smile widened. 'That's my girl.'

'I'm not your girl,' she said, even as unease slithered through her blood.

'Aren't you?' He took a step forwards. 'I like your confidence.'

She didn't retreat, not even when the doctor advanced, his hands still held out to his sides, that ring catching the light and flashing in her eyes. For a second, flames replaced the databanks, a giant wall crashing towards her.

Subria shook her head, and sometime in the microscopic blink of her eyelids, Temple moved. One moment he was three meters away, more than enough for her to see him coming, more than enough time to react, and then he was there, breathing in her face.

Adrenlin hit her system, surged through her veins on the surge of her heart.

Time slowed, and that thing in the back of her brain *clicked*.

Before the thought formed, muscles clenched, tendons flexed, and her fist slammed under Temple's chin.

His head snapped back, even as pain rocketed through her knuckles, rang in her bones, muted and grey, buried under the *click*.

She ducked, spun, lashed out with her boot.

CRACK.

A strangled yell as Temple's knee shattered.

Rise, half a step back, the pistol coming up in the same movement. Her eye on the sight, tracing the bright red crosshair to the spot at the base of his neck, the one that would sever the nerves between brain and body. Temple on his hands and knees, pain lining his face, the tightening of his jaw, giving his complexion a new, pale cast. A sound, a wet strangled laugh followed by the sharp *splat* as he spit blood on the ground.

'No,' he said as he sat back on his heels. 'Not my girl. But perhaps not Kylian's either.'

She ignored him.

'Don't move,' she said.

Temple turned. He stared down the sight, capturing her gaze through the crosshair. He wasn't smiling anymore, his dark face sombre, and something in his gaze.... The *click* sounded in her brain, deep and sharp. Her heart sped, her palms growing warm with the increased blood flow, the scent of dust and the musk of biogel rich in her nose, as that gaze reached through the pistol's sight to grab hold of the thing in her middle.

This wasn't right. The words rang in her head, a warning carried in the beat of her heart and the smooth, steady motion of her lungs.

Focus on the 'pard.

She firmed her stance. 'Don't move,' she said again.

'Maybe you're your mother's girl.' He shifted his weight, preparing to stand, and unease surged a second time, but it wasn't the movement, it was his words. He moved as if it hurt, one hand braced on the knee she hadn't dislocated.

'Maybe I'm just all me,' Subria said.

He laughed, and the unease thickened. 'No, Ms Venere, you have a little bit of something else in there. Trust me.'

'Trust the man raiding the genebanks?' Instructor Bayard's voice rang through the room. 'You're asking a bit much of my recruit.' A shadow moved between the databanks, and the instructor appeared out of the darkness.

'Are you sure she's just a recruit, Ursula?'

'What else would she be? A 'pard?'

'Perhaps. She has the pitiless stare down. Pointy teeth would complete the look.'

'You should have left well enough alone, Temple.'

He stood, groaning as he shifted his weight, not quite straightening all the way. 'I couldn't, you of all people know that.'

'I had hope.'

'You know how I feel about hope.'

'I do.'

There was a beat of silence, time for Subria to hear the blood rush in her ears, the pulse of electricity through the gene banks. Time to watch Temple grip his ring, to see light flash on the metal as he twisted it.

Pain erupted in her ears.

CHAPTER FIVE

Fire raged through the databanks. Ghostly, unreal. Hell-ish.

Subria ran, feeling its hot breath on her neck, the lick of it on her cheek and smelling the awful, acrid stench of burning hair. Oh, God. Not her hair, not her hair. Not. Her. Hair.

Focus on the 'pard. Her daddy's voice played in her ear, took the ragged gasp out of her breathing. Air still rasped and raged in her throat, drew the taste of blood to her tongue and made her lungs burn, but panic no longer choked her.

Running wouldn't get her out of this.

A door up ahead, the flames glinting on plasglas.

She darted right. Slammed her hand into the control pad. The door opened. She squeezed through, hitting the pad on the other side before it was fully open.

The door closed, but she was already ducking, squeezing into the darkest shadow she could find, breath still ragged, heart still thumping, the sense of unreality sticking to her skin.

The flame drew closer, the crackle and rush of it echoing through the walls, lighting up the shadows, heating the air and stealing the sweat from her brow. She could feel it through the steelcrete now, in the floor.

Her heart beat harder.

Her breath came shorter.

Panic bubbled up in her gut, reaching hot sticky tendrils for her reason.

Focus on the 'pard, little tiger. Her dad was in her ear. The floor was no longer steelcrete but the soft loam of an old park, abandoned in the dark reaches of Cumulus City, the knotted branches of ancient trees twisted overhead, naked of leaves, cracking and creaking in the icy breeze, while the musty scent of death filled her nose.

She held the air in her lungs. Let it out, recalled the weight of the rifle in her hands, the smooth cold barrel, the hard curve of the stock against her shoulder.

'Wait for him to come out of the shadows,' her dad whispered in her earpiece. 'Always make him come to you, never go after him.'

'I remember,' she'd whispered back, the words barely enough to ruffle the air, but enough for the comms in the biocomp around her throat to pick up.

'Good. Patience is the watchword and caution is your ally. You might think you have him cornered, but the 'pard is not stupid, not even clouded by his rage.'

'He's rabid, Daddy.'

'That does not make him any less cunning, little tiger; it only makes him thirst for your blood.'

A shadow moved within the darkness, a piece of the night as tall as a man and twice as wide detaching itself from the gloom. It moved slowly, paws bigger than her face, bigger than her whole chest, gliding through the leaf litter, and Subria swore she could feel every step through the soles of her boots. Could feel it vibrating through the soil, echoing with her heart.

Boom. Boom. Boom.

Her breath shuddered.

'I see him, Daddy.'

'I know. Calm.' His breath travelled through the comms, in through the nose, out through the mouth.

Her lungs followed suit.

'Focus,' he said.

She focused, no longer feeling the rifle in her hands, the stock against her shoulder. Seeing only the shadow moving through the dead trees, the giant hulk emerging from the darkness, into her sight.

Focus.

Breathe.

A hum of power, and her HUD snapped into place, and now she could see more of the shadow, the dense black fur, matted and patchy around his chest. The dark river of old blood running down his shoulder from where the other Farm Control unit had shot him. Dried now, like the blood on his muzzle from when he'd torn out the Control officer's throat.

Her HUD scanned the beast as he lumbered out of his hidey-hole, matching ears and chest-size to the warrant sitting on her biocomp, the one that said this companion was hers to kill. The scanner went to work, looking for the tag in his neck. Her finger crept towards the trigger.

'Patience,' her dad said, as if he could see through the distance and the dark, or read her mind, to feel the fear and anticipation riding her nerves. 'You need to confirm the warrant before the kill.'

She didn't need confirmation; the blood and the bullet hole were enough to tell her that this was the one. The human-killer.

'Patience,' he said again.

Patience.

She took her finger off the trigger. Waited as her HUD continued to scan the 'pard. A second ticked by. Another. And another.

Patience.

The 'pard lifted his muzzle, light gleaming off the slick black of his nose. His nostrils expanded, drawing the scents of the park into his lungs, tasting them.

On her HUD, the scan continued, leaving the thick muscles of his neck, travelling down the long, lithe length of his torso, down his flanks to the point of his tail. Nothing. It started back the other way.

The 'pard paused, every muscle in his body freezing before he reared onto his hind legs and breathed again.

'Daddy.' It wasn't even a word, just a twitch of her vocal cords as new tension gripped her body.

'Hold, little tiger.'

Hold. Hold. Hold. The memory rang in her head, over and over as the fire raged on the other side of the plasglas wall. Heating the floor, the air, her lungs. The sound of it vibrating against her skin, the harsh red core turning the shadows into the pits of Hell and burning everything else.

Hold, little tiger.

'Hold,' she whispered. She counted her heart, the ragged thumps, the rush of blood in her ears. One. Two. Th-Three. Four.

Closed her eyes against the black and red of the Hell-scape around her. Concentrated.

One.

Two.

Three.

Tension left her shoulders, unwound from her back, just a little, just enough that her muscles were no longer trying to rip themselves apart.

Enough for her to seek the place inside herself, the oasis where nothing could touch her.

Four.

Five.

Her heart slowed, not all the way, not to where it should, but a measure of calm settled over her mind. Adrenalin still pumped through her veins, but it was no longer the fire of panic, no longer made her hands shake or her breath come in rasps. And now, as she opened her eyes and took in the Hell-scape, she could peel back the sticky sense of unreality and see.

Really see.

Subria crawled out of her shadow.

Flames still cast the lab in shades of red and black, still made the primitive space deep in her mind scream in terror, but it no longer controlled her.

She stood, just enough to peer over the workbench and through the clear plasglas walls.

Her eyes didn't want to focus, wanted to jump left and right and anywhere but the heart of the inferno waiting outside. She grabbed hold of that part of herself, gritted her teeth and forced herself to *see*.

To see the fire standing there. Staring back at her.

She found the pistol.

Stood.

Aimed.

Patience, her daddy whispered. *Confirm the warrant.*

Except there was no HUD this time, no biocomp wrapped around her throat. No warrant. Just Temple on the opposite side of the plasglas, the worm wriggling through his gaze, trying to find its way into her soul.

Her finger found the depression in the grip even as a prayer fell from her lips. She activated the weapon and the barrel assembled itself out of the blackness at the top.

Temple frowned. Cocked his head. His mouth moved, but she didn't hear the words, only felt the stickiness reaching for her.

He wasn't talking to her, and even if he was, the plasglas was too thick for her to hear.

Too thick for sound. Too thick for projectiles.

The panic at the back of her mind still gibbering, Subria moved until she could see the control panel.

Temple's lips didn't stop, and he never took his eyes off her, not even when he did something to the ring on his finger and a holoscreen bloomed above it.

The lab door opened a fraction. Flames leapt, licking at the gap, long orange-blue fingers wrapping around the frame, heat blasting her in the face. The primitive thing screamed, and her grip on it loosened, just for a second, long enough for her heart to leap and a cry to escape her lips.

Hold, little tiger.

Hold.

A breath, a ragged, desperate lunge for the last bit of her control.

She held onto her sanity with the shredded remnants of reason.

The door opened more, and the flames rushed in, pushing the plasglas aside, taking over her vision.

Someone was screaming, the sound loud and high. Piercing.

She stumbled back. One hasty, shaky step, and another. Hands spasming on the pistol as the little bit of sanity left tried to stay in control.

Heat blasted her, boiled the sweat from her skin, seared the hairs from her arms. Roasted her flesh.

A bench slammed into her back. She wanted to crawl over it, wanted to run, wanted to find the closest shadow and hide. Hide. Hide. Hide.

The flames spoke. Words that burned in her ears. Meanings that tried to make it to her brain but pinged off the adrenalin riding her blood.

Now!

The word blasted through her, a shockwave riding all the way down her shoulder, her arm. The pistol *cracked*.

The inferno paused. Wavered.

Silence. A heartbeat for the deep, ragged sound of her breathing echoing in her ears. The roar of the fire silent.

Her ears rang. And then...and then...

The fire groaned, a long deep sound of pain. It flickered. Fell to its knees.

Subria blinked. Blinked again.

There was something in the flames, a shape, dark and fuzzy at first. Human.

She blinked a third time.

The flames died.

Temple knelt on the cold steelcrete, his dark face ashen, his hand, the one with the ring, clamped to his shoulder. He looked at her, but his gaze was fuzzy, unfocused, as a river of red ran through his fingers.

Subria's knees wobbled. The shakes traveling up her legs, turning her thighs to jelly, making her stomach jump, skittering down her arms. The pistol wobbled, dipped, the weight of it dragging her down. Not just her arms but every muscle drooping as endorphins replaced adrenalin, relief replaced panic.

It was over.

She hit the floor, not feeling the jolt or the cool surface through her pants.

Over.

Except it wasn't.

A rush of air, the sour smell of old meat and rage, the hot musk of fur.

A scream. Blood gushing across her face.

Her dad. Dying.

There was fog in her brain and she was losing it, the now, the here, losing it to old nightmares. But she was able to lift the pistol, to fire, before she went under.

⊕

She was back in the park, the lab a half-forgotten dream buried under the weight of memory, of the night a ruc-pard tore her dad apart.

The 'pard scenting the air, his black pitiless gaze turning towards the bench she knelt behind. The heavy *thud*, unheard and unfelt but in her imagination as loud as a shuttle landing on her head. The way the 'pard appeared to see through the holo-cloak, to see *her* kneeling in the old loam, still waiting for her HUD to confirm the warrant. Still waiting for her rifle to unlock.

The roar that rattled her bones. The charge.

All of that great, lumbering darkness rushing towards her, a cargo train pushing the scent of old blood and rotting meat ahead of it. Pushing terror.

'The warrant's not confirming, Daddy.' There was a waver in her voice, one that matched the shakes in her legs. 'Daddy!'

'Hold, little tiger.' There was something in her dad's voice, a thread of steel under the usual practiced calm. 'I have you.'

She clutched her rifle, hands sweating. Heart beating hard. Eyes half-focussed on the scan still running over the 'pard, the rest of her... the rest of her fighting not to get up from her crouch and run. Run. Run. Except there was nowhere to run, nowhere close enough, safe enough. No way to outrun the fury and bloodlust getting bigger and bigger in her scope.

Daddy had her.

Daddy had her.

Daddy had her.

A slice of the night screamed out of the trees, diving for the 'pard with talons and teeth. Erebos.

The 'pard swiped at the flyer, sending him barrelling into a tree.

Another slice of darkness, landing with a light thud and crouching atop the bench. Uniform sucking in the light, the glow of his HUD highlighting sharp cheekbones, gleaming off midnight hair. A pistol in his hand.

Daddy.

'Run,' he said.

What? The word wanted to explode out of her chest, but shock held it still.

'Run!' He yelled it this time, anger in his words, in his eyes, in the lines of his face.

She stumbled upright, took two shaky steps backward as her daddy turned to the 'pard. Started firing.

The 'pard kept coming, the shots from her dad's pistol sinking into the dark fur of its chest, but not slowing it. It was only metres from them now, a few bounds.

Daddy was rising, jumping off the bench, moving backwards, never taking his eyes off the killing machine hurtling towards them.

But he took a moment to glance at her. 'Subria!'

She ran.

The boundary of the park was ahead, a high wall separating dead grass from the landing pad and their shuttle.

If she could get there, she could get the other weapons, the ones that weren't—

A roar. A scream.

Subria spun back around.

The 'pard threw her dad in the air.

He tumbled, arms and legs spinning. Slammed into the ground.

Didn't move.

No. Please God, no.

'Dad!'

The 'pard roared again. Pounced.

Her HUD picked out the white flash of its claws, the spray of blood. Found the chip in the beast's ruined shoulder.

Another scream. Her dad flipped on his belly. Crawling.

The rifle was still in her hands.

The warrant blinked blue. *Kill warrant approved,* it said.

She was on one knee, the other steadying the rifle as she raised and sighted down the barrel.

The 'pard looked up. Saw her. Roared.

Her HUD screamed warnings in her ears, flashed them across the visor, bright glaring red as the animal charged.

She squeezed the trigger.

She didn't remember the 'pard falling mid-leap, its momentum carrying it through the dirt to rest half a metre from her knees. She didn't remember it twitching, or the burning hole between its eyes. She only remembered stumbling through the dark, lifting her dad into her arms, praying for him to live as the blood ran over his chest.

'I got you, Daddy.'

He smiled.

CHAPTER SIX

There was something in her face, the heavy scent of fish crawling up her nose and down her throat. She turned away, but the smell followed her, tickled her cheeks, and—

The long line of warmth, rough enough to remove skin, jerked her awake.

She was scuttling backwards before her eyes were open, her back smacking up against something hard, head following.

Stars burst in her eyes, made it difficult to focus on the shadow looming over her, but she was already darting sideways, scrambling for her pistol—

'Easy, recruit.' Instructor Bayard's voice rang from somewhere in the mess of lights and shadows fogging her vision. 'It's done.'

Subria blinked, squinted against the lights silhouetting the... Not Bayard, unless the instructor had grown a snout and another four legs since she'd last seen her.

The blue-grey 'pard licked her cheek again.

Subria shoved the animal's snout away, or tried to. Instead she was caught in the 'pard's black gaze, falling, falling, falling all the way to that quiet place. Peace soaked through her pores and into her marrow, while that space behind her heart opened, filling with the scent of rain, the brush of fur and a sense of belonging. Of completeness.

The 'pard rumbled, the sound rising from her chest, filling the air with all of the things Subria could feel in her heart, with a...

connection.

Slowly, the hand raised to push the strider away turned, stretched to cup the companion's jaw. It was soft, warm and silken, a balm to her nerves, soothing the panic and fear.

The companion closed her eyes, the rumble – a purr, Subria realised – growing louder as she leaned into Subria's touch.

A word shivered through Subria's skin, travelling through the nerves where her hand stroked the 'pard. It was fuzzy, as if seen through a dense fog, shivering on the tip of her tongue, almost forming in her mind and dissipating again as she reached for it.

The 'pard pushed her head closer, almost touching Subria's chin with her nose, allowing Subria to reach up and scratch the soft fur behind the companion's ear.

The word grew, the shape of it becoming clearer. Subria leaned forward, resting her forehead against the 'pard's, and reached up with her other hand, arms encircling her head.

Apani. Forest and mountainsides, the fog clinging to the trunks, scattering in the wake of a silent shadow.

'Apani,' she whispered, opening her eyes.

The 'pard, Apani, purred louder.

The space in Subria's chest suddenly grew, expanding until she thought it might explode, filling with the scent of rain, with *Apani* and—

A yowl tore the sensation from Subria's chest. And then shadows and fury were between them, driving the 'pard back with wings and fangs, talons flashing in the lights. Air rushed backed into Subria's lungs, a great shuddering mouthful as the space in her chest collapsed, the rain replaced with the musk of fur and the copper tang of blood.

Subria sucked it down, even as she shot to her feet, trying to make sense of what had just happened.

The 'pard was growling, low rippling snarls, trying to dodge Erberos, to catch Subria's gaze again, but the flyer was liquid darkness, always in Apani's way, always—

'Enough.' Instructor Bayard was there, somehow between the 'pard and Erberos, reaching out to snatch the flyer from the air, but he slipped out of her grasp, somersaulting through the air to land on Subria's shoulder.

The 'pard shook her head and took a pace forward, snarling.

Erberos mantled his wings, snarling back.

'Look at her,' Bayard spoke to the 'pard.

The 'pard's gaze switched from Erberos to her, and Subria shrank from it.

The 'pard's snarl died.

'You'll have to wait,' Bayard said again.

The companion chuffed, cocked her head, and, eyes never leaving Subria's, backed out of the lab.

The door slid shut between them.

CHAPTER SEVEN

Silence ruled the shuttle, save for the soft rustle of feathers and the gentle hum of a sternard's breathing.

Subria sat at the front of the main cabin, away from the recruits with their new companions, unable to take her eye from the sternard sprawled across the near aisle, its giant head on Sheera's knee. It looked nothing like Yaara, a chocolate brown monstrosity with darker plating across its chest, and yet she could not shake the fear that slithered through her veins, the memory of Yaara's blood-stained muzzle, her handler torn apart.

A gentle hum and Erebos bumped his head into her jaw, his scales warm against her skin, his body a comforting weight on her shoulder, his talons a reassuring prick through the nano-leather of her jacket.

She'd saved her classmates, stopped Doctor Temple from hacking the gene banks, and yet she'd failed. Only two of the eight recruits who had taken the shuttle to the Farm found companions; the rest of them... At least there wouldn't be much to pack once she returned to the academy, and there'd be no need to comm her mum or her sister to pick her up. Just a taxi, and the silent walk to the front door.

If she was quick, she'd be able to get her application in for Sabre University before the first trimester started.

On her shoulder, Erebos hissed.

Subria looked up as Bayard took the bench next to her.

'Your father would have been proud.'

'You knew him?'

The instructor laughed. 'Everyone knew Kylian Venere, and those that didn't have the chance know your mother.' The humour on her face faded, and for a moment she stared out into the distance, her brow furrowed and her mouth pinched as if in remembered pain. 'The Venere name is a lot to live up to.'

Subria nodded, just once, even as shame curled in her chest. There were other ways to live up to the family name, she told herself. Other careers, and yet the thought did nothing for the bitterness winding through her soul.

'I'm going to push you hard, Venere. There's no room for people who coast on their family name at Morague, only hard work and blood.'

'What?' She sat up, the meaning of Bayard's words slipping past the shame. 'But... ' Her voice trailed off.

'You didn't return to the shuttle with a companion?' Bayard finished for her. She eyed Erebos. 'Or a second one, at least.'

The instructor grunted. 'Never fails to amaze me how many of you believe we'd throw away a promising recruit because they didn't bond with a strider. Even if we did, your actions in stopping Doctor Temple would have earned you a place.'

Bayard leaned back against the bulkhead. 'The test wasn't the striders, girl, it was the forest, the sky.'

'The Pollen,' Subria breathed. 'You wanted to see if we would panic, like Bank.'

'Mm hmm. There's always a few.'

'But why the striders?'

A smile lifted the corner of Bayard's mouth. 'Because if I hadn't, you'd all have been looking for the real test and have had a chance to brace yourselves. Besides, every rider needs a strider, and this is convenient.'

'Tyvian and Sheera have a head start, but real bonds are formed over time, girl.' Bayard nodded towards the rear of the compartment, where Sheera stared into her sterdane's eyes and

Tyvian stroked his pea-dragon's wings as if the huge companion would fly away if he stopped.

'You can put that down to the right combination of pheromones and timing. Love at first sight, if you will, but in the end their bond won't be any stronger than the one you forge.

'Now, if one of them caught the attention of a Woolsey…' Bayard's black gaze locked on Subria, stayed there. 'Well, that would have been different.'

It took effort not to shift on the bench, to keep her face blank and meet Bayard's stare as the memory of the blue-grey 'pard played behind her eyeballs, the…the *thing* that had passed between them. Subria fought the urge to rub her chest, to soothe the small, hollow space left behind.

Erebos landed on her knees, his outspread wings a wall of darkness breaking the stare.

Subria breathed.

Erebos folded his wings, one set at a time, and glided up her arm to rest on her shoulder. She scratched the little hollow at the base of his head, where skull met spine, grateful for the distraction.

The wan-adder hummed, eyes open, attention fixed, not on Subria, but on the instructor.

Bayard sat forward, elbows on her knees, returning Erebos's regard.

The 'adder growled.

Bayard bared her teeth. 'You can't keep her from it forever.'

Erebos hissed, fangs flashing.

The instructor laughed, the sound as dark as Erebos's hide, and stood. 'You'll need bigger teeth before you can scare me, little shadow. And you.' She pointed at her, and Subria wondered how a single, work-roughed finger could be so intimidating. 'I'll have you sorted out before the end of the first trimester. Mark my words.' She clasped Subria's shoulder. 'Welcome to the Academy.'

AUTHOR'S NOTE

May 2020

I suck at prequels.

When I started writing *Hunter*, the goal was to create a quick little introduction to The Hero Rebellion trilogy. It was meant to be a short self-contained story, something to help new readers discover the series and a bonus for fans, but I realised very quickly that wasn't going to happen.

This sucker had a mind of its own.

Instead of a Hero Rebellion prequel, I present to you a prequel to a prequel series (which I guess makes me really good at prequels??). And yes, you read it right, Subria is getting her own series. Apani and Ursula will be there, as well as Norah's grandfather and a few other characters you might remember.

When will you be getting this as yet unnamed series? Currently, I'm slated to start work on it after I finish The Hero War series, which should be the end of 2021.

I know, I know, that's like forever away, but there's a lot happening between now and then, including the conclusion to The Echo trilogy and then The Hero War. So, make sure to stay in touch!

DO YOU WANT MORE HERO?

I love keeping in touch with my readers, it's the second-best thing about being a writer (writing being the first best). Every fortnight (or thereabouts), I send out a newsletter with details about upcoming offers, new releases and extra special projects.

If you sign up for the mailing you'll receive exclusive behind-the-scenes extras, such as:

- free short stories
- deleted and alternate scenes from The Hero Rebellion
- previews of my upcoming books
- pancakes
- quizes
- and much, much more!

Sign up here
news.belindacrawford.com/newsletter

ABOUT THE AUTHOR

Physics makes Belinda's brain hurt, while quadratics cause her eyes to cross and any mention of probability equations will have her running for the door. Nonetheless, she loves watching documentaries about the natural world, biology, space, history and technology.

She's also a sucker for a fast horse, a faster computer and superhero movies. When she's not doing the horse, computer or superhero thing, Belinda writes science fiction (emphasis on the fiction), where she loves to write about butt-kicking girls who blow stuff up.

You can keep in touch with Belinda, or just pick her brains about sci-fi via her website, Facebook or by sending her an email (she loves email).

www.belindacrawford.com
belinda@belindacrawford.com

Have news delivered straight to your inbox
via her mailing list. Sign up at:
news.belindacrawford.com/newsletter